THE WAILING WALL

If I forget thee, O Jerusalem...
—Psalms 137:5

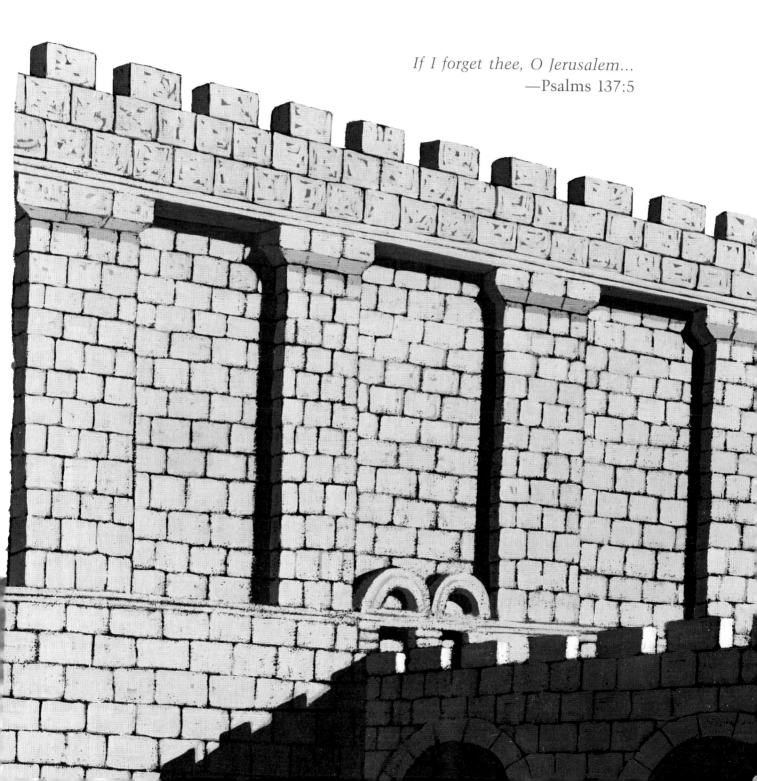

THE WAILING WALL

LEONARD EVERETT FISHER

MACMILLAN PUBLISHING COMPANY   NEW YORK

COLLIER MACMILLAN PUBLISHERS   LONDON

CHRONOLOGY OF THE FIRST AND SECOND TEMPLES, CIRCA 1900 B.C. – 1967

1900 – – Abraham comes to Canaan from Ur, Mesopotamia. Near sacrifice of Isaac takes place on Mt. Moriah in Salem.

1900–1600 – – Jacob (Israel) fathers twelve sons: Reuben, Simeon, Levi, Judah, Zebulun, Issachar, Dan, Gad, Asher, Naphtali, Joseph, Benjamin.

1500 – – Salem becomes Jerusalem, City of Peace.

1600–1200 – – Hebrew tribes live in Egypt.

1200–1160 – – Hebrews depart Egypt, wander the desert, and reenter Canaan.

1160–1000 – – Hebrews conquer Jesubites. Philistines are defeated. King David makes Jerusalem the capital and places the Ark of the Covenant on Mt. Moriah.

961 – – King Solomon completes the building of the First Temple.

922 – – Hebrew tribes divide into two nations: Israel and Judah.

701 – – Assyrians conquer Israel.

587–538 – – Nebuchadnezzar destroys the First Temple. Jews are sent to Babylonia.

538–515 – – Jews return to Jerusalem and complete the building of the Second Temple.

332 – – Alexander the Great conquers Jerusalem.

167 – – Persians make the Second Temple a pagan shrine.

167–164 – – Jews defeat Persians and rededicate the Second Temple.

63 – – Rome occupies Jerusalem.

37–24 – – Herod the Great is made King of Judaea and remodels the Second Temple.

4 – – Jesus is born. Herod orders the Massacre of the Innocents. Herod dies.

0 – – The modern calendar begins.

29 – – Jesus is arrested, tried, condemned, executed.

66–70 – – Jews revolt against Romans. Romans destroy the Second Temple.

570 – – Mohammed, founder of Islam, the Moslem religion, is born.

638–691 – – Moslems take Jerusalem and build the Mosque of Omar on Mt. Moriah.

1096–1291 – – Christians attempt the conquest of the "Holy Land."

1917 – – Great Britain takes Jerusalem and Palestine from Moslem Turks.

1948 – – State of Israel is reestablished by the United Nations. The Wailing Wall remains in Moslem East Jerusalem.

1967 – – Israel defeats Arab armies in Six Day War. Israel occupies East Jerusalem and repossesses the Wailing Wall.

The decorations in this book belong to the history of the Middle East. They are a menorah and a Star of David, symbols of Jewish faith; the Babylonian sun god, Samash; a Persian coin; a Greek helmet; a Roman eagle; a Christian cross; and the Islamic crescent and star.

Macmillan Publishing Company, 866 Third Avenue, New York, NY 10022. Collier Macmillan Canada, Inc.
First Edition   Printed in the United States of America

10   9   8   7   6   5   4   3   2   1

The text of this book was set in 14 pt. Trump Medieval. The black-and-white paintings were rendered in acrylic paints on paper.

Library of Congress Cataloging-in-Publication Data
Fisher, Leonard Everett. The Wailing Wall. Summary: Surveys the history of the Jewish people in Palestine and their activities around the First and Second Temples, the site of which is now marked by the Western or Wailing Wall, with an emphasis on events before 70 A.D. 1. Bible. O.T.—History of Biblical events—Pictorial works—Juvenile literature. 2. Jews—History—To 70 A.D.—Pictorial works—Juvenile literature. 3. Western Wall (Jerusalem)—Pictorial works—Juvenile literature. [1. Jews—History—To 70 A.D. 2. Palestine—History—To 70 A.D. 3. Western Wall (Jerusalem)] I. Title.
BS539.F57 1989 221.9′5 88-27192 ISBN 0-02-735310-9

With appreciation to Dr. Michael Stanislawski, Professor of History, Columbia University

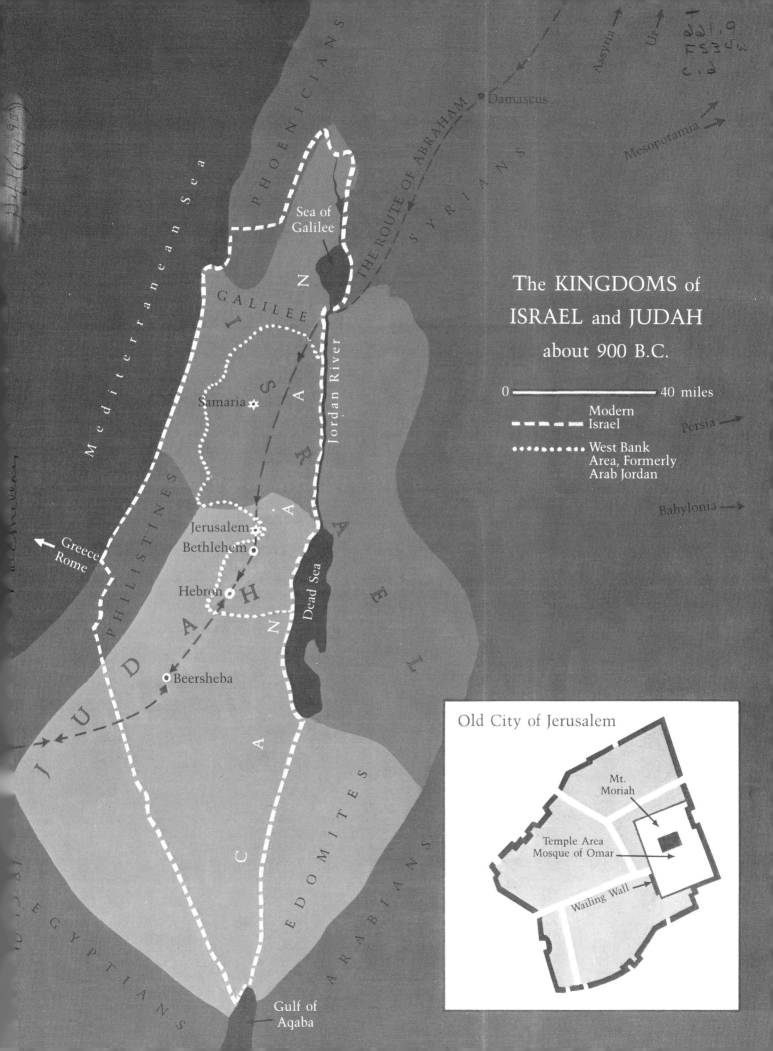

The KINGDOMS of
ISRAEL and JUDAH
about 900 B.C.

0 ———————————— 40 miles

– – – – Modern
Israel

• • • • • • • • West Bank
Area, Formerly
Arab Jordan

Damascus

Assyria
Ur
Mesopotamia
Persia
Babylonia

S Y R I A N S

THE ROUTE OF ABRAHAM

P H O E N I C I A N S

Mediterranean Sea

Sea of
Galilee

G A L I L E E

I
S
R
A
E
L

Jordan River

N

Samaria

Jerusalem
Bethlehem

Hebron

Dead Sea

Greece
Rome

P H I L I S T I N E S

J
U
D
A
H

Beersheba

C A N A A N

E D O M I T E S

A R A B I A N S

E G Y P T I A N S

Gulf of
Aqaba

Old City of Jerusalem

Mt.
Moriah

Temple Area
Mosque of Omar

Wailing Wall

An ancient stone wall stands in Jerusalem, Israel. It rises forty feet above ground and stretches one hundred sixty feet. It is the remains of an outer wall of the Second Temple, which was built by the Jews nearly twenty-five hundred years ago and later destroyed. Twenty feet below ground are stone rows from the First Temple, built about four hundred fifty years earlier.

Jews from around the world visit these stones to weep over the Temple's destruction and to seek God's favor. Called the Western, or "Wailing," Wall, these blocks represent nearly four thousand years of Jewish history that began with Abraham the Hebrew.

Abraham settled in the land of Canaan, now modern Israel. There, in the town of Salem, he made a covenant, or "agreement," with God. He promised that he and his descendants would worship only Him. To prove his faith, he took his son Isaac to Mount Moriah to be sacrificed. But Isaac was spared.

One of Isaac's sons, Jacob, called Israel, had twelve sons who began their own families, or "tribes." Famine and drought drove them all south to Egypt, where they were later enslaved. After four hundred years of living in Egypt and forty years of wandering in the desert, they returned to Canaan and became one kingdom, Israel.

When Saul, their first king, died fighting the Philistines, a former shepherd boy named David became king. David made old Salem—now Jerusalem, City of Peace—his capital. And on the spot where Abraham had nearly sacrificed Isaac, he pitched a tent, or "Tabernacle," to house the Ark of the Covenant. The Ark was a special chest made of wood and gold. It held the Ten Commandments—the "Law"—and served to remind the Israelites of Abraham's agreement. As trumpets blared and David danced, the Ark was placed inside the Tabernacle. To the Israelites, this became the holiest site on earth.

Around 961 B.C. David's son, King Solomon, replaced the Tabernacle with the First Temple. It was a great building made of stone, brick, wood, silver, and gold. The people were very pleased with their temple. They were not altogether happy with their king, however, because his wives worshiped many gods.

The unhappy Israelites divided about forty years later. Ten tribes formed the northern kingdom of Israel, whose capital was Samaria. Two tribes formed the southern kingdom of Judah. The northerners continued to call themselves Israelites. The southerners called themselves Judeans, or "Jews." Jerusalem, once the capital of a single nation and home of the First Temple, was now the capital of Judah.

The Kingdom of Israel lasted two hundred twenty-one years. A ferocious Assyrian army swept out of the east and destroyed it. The surviving Israelites disappeared, becoming known as the "Lost Tribes of Israel."

The Judeans thrived until 587 B.C., when Nebuchadnezzar II of Babylonia hurled his army against them. Jerusalem and the First Temple were left in ruins. Gone, too, was the Ark of the Covenant. Most Jews were exiled to Babylonia, where they remained for half a century.

Nebuchadnezzar soon went mad. He thought he was an ox and loped in the fields, eating grass. Babylonia, now no longer a feared and powerful nation, was captured by King Cyrus of Persia in 538 B.C. Cyrus let the Jews return to Jerusalem, where, in 515 B.C., they finished building the Second Temple on the wreckage of the first.

The Jews rebuffed invaders for two centuries. Finally, in 332 B.C. a Greek general called Alexander the Great over-whelmed them and took Jerusalem. For the next one hundred sixty-seven years the Greeks, together with their Egyptian and Syrian allies, ruled Judah.

Neither the Greeks nor the Egyptians prevented the Jews from praying to one God in the Second Temple. But the Syrians, who believed in Greek gods and goddesses and prayed to their statues, decided to use the Second Temple to worship Zeus, king of the Greek gods. In 167 B.C. they forced the Jews to pray to Zeus and murdered those who refused.

The Jews were furious. They had worshiped God on that holy ground for more than eight hundred years. Now they were ousted by statue worshipers. They revolted and fought the Syrians for three years—from 167 to 164 B.C. Led by Judas Maccabaeus, they drove the Syrians from Jerusalem. The victorious Jews rededicated their Second Temple to God. The celebration was called Hanukkah, the Hebrew word for "dedication."

But then the Jews began to quarrel with one another. Some believed that their centuries-old Torah—the written record of their beginnings, Abraham's agreement, the Ten Commandments, and much more of their history—should be their only guide. Others felt that since times had changed, they needed new laws to live by. In 63 B.C. a Roman army took advantage of the quarreling and occupied Judah. Jerusalem fell. Judah became Judaea, a Roman province.

The Romans made Herod the Great, an Edomite, King of Judaea. Herod dreamed of ruling an empire with splendid buildings. About 24 B.C. he remodeled the Second Temple, turning it into a dazzling structure that looked more like a Roman palace than a Jewish house of worship.

Herod was as ruthless as he was vain. In Bethlehem the new-born son of Joseph and Mary, whose name was Joshua—Jesus in Greek—was being hailed as "King of the Jews." Fearful of losing his crown, Herod ordered that all the baby boys of Bethlehem be killed. But Joseph, Mary, and the infant Jesus escaped.

As a young man, Jesus roamed Judaea, telling the Jews that a "new kingdom" was close at hand. The Jews wanted only to be free of the Romans and the Herods. Some saw Jesus as the Messiah, their savior. Others thought Jesus was a meddler because he wanted to change the old customs. In Jerusalem, for example, Jesus drove money changers and dove sellers from the Temple grounds. He believed it was too sacred a place to be used for such common practices.

Both Romans and Jews felt that Jesus had become a threat to their authority. Moreover, Herod Antipas, governor of Galilee and son of Herod the Great, wanted to succeed his father as King of Judaea. The Romans had named no one king. Jesus was brought before the Romans for claiming to be King of the Jews and for promising the Jews a "new kingdom." He was tried, condemned, and executed for treason.

In 66 the Jews revolted. Nero, the Roman emperor, sent his strongest general, Vespasian, to put down the uprising. While Vespasian fought the Jews, Nero died. Vespasian returned to Rome in 69 to become the new emperor. He put his oldest son, Titus, in command of the legions in Judaea.

The following year, 70, Titus crushed the Jews. He destroyed the Second Temple and hauled back to Rome Jewish slaves and their Temple treasures. All that was left of the Second Temple was a piece of its outer western wall. Try as they might, the Romans could not budge the massive blocks.

For the next five hundred years Romans—at first pagans, then Christians—ruled Judaea. Countless Jews lived elsewhere in the world, in exile, waiting to reclaim their homeland.

In 638 Moslem horsemen rode out of the desert and conquered Jerusalem. Fifty-three years later the Mosque of Omar, or Dome of the Rock, a Moslem house of worship, rose where the First and Second Temples once had stood. What was left of the Western Wall remained standing, untouched, immovable.

MORE ABOUT THE WAILING WALL

For centuries Moslems and Christians fought each other for Jerusalem, the Holy City. At times Jews were barred not only from their sacred wall, but also from Jerusalem. Beginning in the 1880s, however, they began to return in large numbers to their ancient land, then called Palestine.

In 1917 a British army with Jewish units defeated the Moslem Turks in Palestine and took Jerusalem. Great Britain governed Palestine until 1948, when the United Nations reestablished the independent State of Israel. But Jerusalem was divided between two countries, Israel and Arab Jordan. And the Wailing Wall was on the Jordanian side. Again Jews were forbidden to visit the Wailing Wall. Even the Jewish victory over an attacking Arab army in 1948 did not help them to regain access to it.

In 1967 Israel once more defeated Arab armies. This time Israel occupied the section of Jerusalem that included the Wailing Wall. Once more Jews could journey to their holy site to weep over the destruction of the Second Temple, and to rejoice in the rebirth of the Jewish nation.